MASHED MYTHS!

GREEK HEROES

Andrew Traucki & Mick Wannenmacher

NYC Press
5050 Romaine St #12
Los Angeles, CA, 90029
USA
www.nyc-press.com
nycpress@nyc-press.com

Library of Congress Cataloging-in-Publication Data:

Traucki, Andrew
Wannenmacher, Mick

MASHED MYTHS: Greek Heroes/Andrew Traucki & Mick Wannenmacher

ISBN: 978-0-9600481-0-6 (paperback)
Library of Congress Control Number: 2018965552

-WANTED-

HERO

MUST BE:

Brave

Willing to fight monsters

Have own sword

Ok with possible gruesome death

*Being a child of a god an advantage
but not a requirement

IF THIS IS YOU, APPLY IN PERSON OR BY WINGED HORSE TO:

THE ORACLE OF DELPHI

102 Golden Fleece Way

Ancient Greece

800 BC

*Minotaurs need not apply

HERO WANTED HERO WANTED HERO WANTED HERO WANTED HERO WANTED HERO WANTED

ARE YOU AN ANCIENT GREEK HERO?

Take our unscientifically proven quiz to FIND OUT!!!

INSTRUCTIONS:

Add up the points from your answers and see if you're an ANCIENT GREEK HERO!

If you could choose any pet, it would be:

(a) A magical flying horse (8 points)

(b) A snail (2 points)

(c) A fire-breathing dragon (6 points)

(d) A cat called Puss Puss McPusskins (4 points)

On the weekend you like to get around in:

(a) A yellow onesie (4 points)

(b) Gleaming golden armour (8 points)

(c) Nothing. Totally nude! Eeek! (6 points)

(d) Shorts and a t-shirt (2 points)

Your idea of having fun is:

(a) Hunting dragons (6 points)

(b) Cleaning your room (4 points)

(c) Shooting flaming arrows at
a giant, eight tentacled, bug-eyed
monster (8 points)

(d) Watching ads on TV (2 points)

To see if you've got what it takes to be an
Ancient Greek Hero, add up your score!

6 - 12 points: You are a cuddly teddy bear.

13 - 17 points: You are still a
cuddly teddy bear, but a very
fierce one.

18 - 24 points: Go grab your sword,
armor and get yourself to Ancient
Greece RIGHT NOW! You are 129%
ANCIENT GREEK HERO!!!!

Inside This Book

MASHED MYTHS

Myths are magical stories that explain special things like gods, thunder, volcanoes, and marshmallow bunnies.*

(*probably not marshmallow bunnies)

Since ancient times, people have been telling these stories to help them make sense of the world.

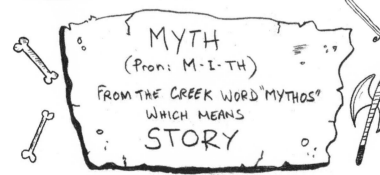

MYTH
(Pron: M-I-TH)

FROM THE GREEK WORD "MYTHOS"
WHICH MEANS
STORY

BUT WHO WANTS TO DO THAT?!? Here at Mashed Myths we have mashed, mangled, and messed up these tales for laughs. And hey, if you really want to read the original stories — go do your own research!

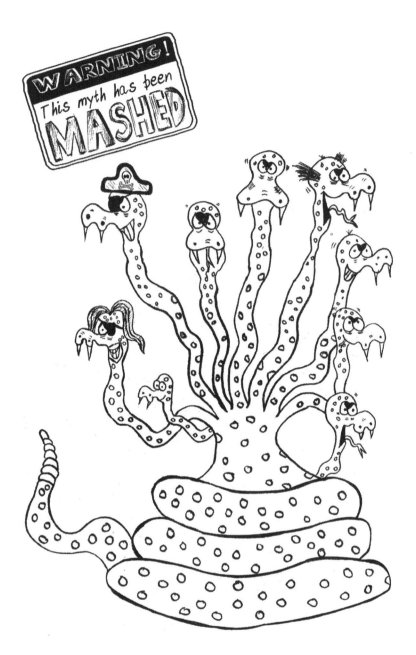

Tale the First
Hercules & the Hydra
PART I

Hercules was a hero. One of the greatest ever. He was very strong, extremely brave, and had great hair. Like, seriously great. He could have been in a shampoo commercial, except he lived in Ancient

Greece and they didn't have TV back then. Or shampoo. But you get the idea.

Hercules had to serve the king of Tiryns. I won't go into why because it's pretty gruesome. (Hint: he kind of, sort of, accidentally killed a lot of people.)

Before he was allowed to go free, the king gave Hercules twelve tasks to complete.

Now, twelve tasks doesn't seem like that many. But the king was afraid of Hercules (see previous note about Hercules killing people). So instead of giving him jobs like walking the dog or cleaning the toilet, he gave Hercules twelve extremely dangerous jobs to do, like, *crazy* dangerous, hoping that Hercules would get killed doing them. (Though cleaning the toilet can be very dangerous, especially after your dad's been in there.)

The king told Herc to go kill the savage Nemean Lion. Not only did Hercules kill it, he wore it as a hat! (But only when he was having a bad hair day.)

The king was furious that Hercules had survived (and now had a cool hat), so he thought of an even more dangerous task: Kill the nine-headed Hydra monster that lived in the nearby Swamp of Lerna.

"Righto," said Hercules. "Piece of cake."

"Yep," said his nephew Iolaus, who was driving him to the swamp in his chariot. "Piece of cake. If by 'cake' you mean 'enormous nine-headed, super-fast, super-strong snake with hundreds of razor-sharp teeth dripping with deadly poison.' That sort of cake?"

Piece of cake ←

Not a piece of cake →

A muffin (irrelevant) →

"Very funny," grumbled Hercules. "I wish you'd be a bit more positive."

"I am positive," said Iolaus as he pulled the chariot to a stop. "I am positive you are going to get eaten by the Hydra."

HYDRA POOP NOW WITH 100% MORE HERCULES

NEXT 30 Km

"Well," said Iolaus with a grin, "looks like we're here."

They stopped on the edge of a murky pond in the middle of the swamp. Bubbles of swamp gas glooped and popped on its surface. On the other side of the pond was a dark cave. Bones and gigantic snake scales lay scattered about the opening. A low hiss echoed from its black depths and the whole place stunk of rotting flesh and farts.

Hercules stared nervously at the gloomy entrance to the Hydra's lair.

"I'm not going in there!" he squeaked.

"What's your plan then, hero?" said Iolaus. "Wait out here until it dies of old age?"

"No!" snapped Hercules. "I need to draw it out here, where I've got room to fight."

Hercules picked a booger from his nose and flicked it away. It landed on Iolaus.

"Ew! Gross! If you're going to do that, I'm leaving." huffed Iolaus.

Boogerus Grossus

"That's it!" exclaimed Hercules. "I'll shoot something down there to make it angry!"

"Boogers?" said Iolaus. "They might gross it out a bit, but—"

"Fire!" shouted Hercules. "I'll shoot fire arrows down the hole! Snakes hate fire."

"And lizards," said Iolaus. "Cos lizards have legs, and the snakes are jealous."

Hiya!

Ding Ding

But Hercules was no longer listening. He grabbed an arrow from his quiver and wrapped the head in cloth soaked with lamp oil. Lighting the arrow with his lantern, he stretched back the string on his mighty bow.

"Here goes nothing," thought Hercules. *ZHOOM!* A flaming arrow streaked into the cave. The hissing suddenly stopped.

"Do you think it worked?" he said.

But Iolaus didn't answer — the ground beneath them had begun to tremble. The hissing was replaced by a ROAR and the cave mouth shook and shivered as something… something HUGE thundered out of the darkness towards them.

"Yep," gulped Iolaus. "I think it worked."

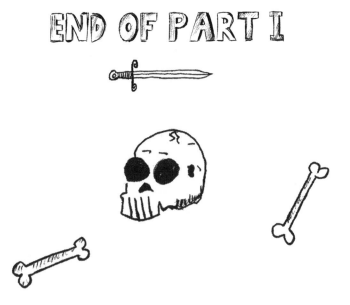

END OF PART I

ANCIENT GREEKS - HUH?

 The Ancient Greeks lived between 800 BCE and 500 BCE. They lived in Greece (duh!), a country in southeastern Europe.

The Ancient Greeks were great thinkers, warriors, writers, actors, athletes, artists, and politicians.

They invented heaps of things we still use today, like the alarm clock, the Olympics, and the fart bomb.*

*Ok, maybe not the fart bomb but I bet they could have.

Hercules & the Hydra
PART II

Previously in Hercules & the Hydra:
Seriously? You need to be told what happened? It was, like, a page ago. One page! Flip back and read it again. Go on... Got it? Good. Now read on.

An enormous snake head burst out of the dark tunnel! It looked around angrily, deadly poison dripping from its giant fangs.

"Oh, it's only got one head," said Iolaus. "That's not so bad."

Pop! Pop! Pop! Pop! Eight more heads suddenly lunged into view. Each head was even uglier and more vicious than the last.

UGLY   UGLIER   UGLIEST

18

"Ah. Right. So what's the plan, Herc? Some piece of brilliant, sneaky trickery?"

"Plan? I'm a hero. This is my plan!" And with that, Hercules roared like a madman and leapt across the swampy pond.

"Good plan!" called out Iolaus. "I'll just stay here then."

Hercules grabbed the Hydra around one of its necks and squeezed. His massive arms were like tree trunks. Muscles like steel stretched and bulged as he tried to squash the gigantic snake. The monster was not going to be beaten that easily though.

It quickly wound its coils around Hercules and squeezed back.

THWACK! Hercules swung his mighty sword and lopped one of the Hydra's heads clean off! It went flying off into the swamp, where it squashed an unlucky frog.

"Ha!" shouted Hercules. "One down! Eight more to… whaaaaaat?!?"

To Hercules's astonishment, TWO terrifying snake heads replaced the head he had just chopped off.

"That's not good," thought Hercules. "Oh well, I'll just have to try harder."

Hercules whirled his sword through the air again and *WHUMPF!* Another head went crashing to the ground (where it squashed another unlucky frog, who had come out to see what had happened to his friend).

But no sooner had the snake head hit the dirt, two more burst out of the neck to replace it! One of the heads lunged forward, nearly taking Hercules's arm off.

"This is not going well!" Hercules shouted. "A little help would be—OW!"

Pain shot through Hercules's foot. Looking down, he saw that a giant crab had crunched its massive claw onto his big toe.

+ ⟨hand⟩ = OWW!!

"Who-ow! Has-ow! A giant crab-OW! For a friend!?" thought Hercules. With a mighty heave, he swung his foot and kicked the crab, hard! *BOOSH!* It went zooming away—STRAIGHT TOWARD IOLAUS!!

WHOOOSH!!!

Iolaus dove to the side but *DONK!* the crab bounced off his head. Iolaus's legs scissored wildly in the air until *BOOT!* his foot connected hard with the flying crab. It shot through the air right between two nearby trees, killing the crab and inventing football at the same time.

"Gooooaaaallll!" shrieked Iolaus. "Did ya see that Hercules?!"

But Hercules had his own problems. As fast as he cut the snake heads off, more and more grew back.

The Hydra now had more than thirty heads, and its massive coils were squeezing Hercules so tight that he kept farting. (Embarrassing AND deadly.) He was keeping the vicious fangs away with his sword (and smelly butt), but only just.

"I've got an idea!" shouted Iolaus. He grabbed an oil-soaked cloth, wrapped it around a stick and lit it on fire. Holding the flaming torch up in front of him, Iolaus raced toward the battle!

(Which is how the Olympic Torch was invented.*)

*This is probably, almost certainly not true.

"IOLAUS! STOP!" shrieked Hercules.

"What is it, Hercules?!" shouted Iolaus.

"Watch out for my hair!" Hercules gasped back. "I've just got it looking really good!"

"Seriously?" said Iolaus. "That's what you're worried about? Just shut up and keep cutting!"

Hercules pulled his arm free of the Hydra's coils and *SWISH!* he sliced his sword through one of the snake's necks. A head went CRASHING to the ground (almost killing another frog.) Iolaus plunged the burning rag against the stump of the neck. With a sizzle, the flesh seared shut. No more heads grew back!

"Woohoo! Keep cutting, Herc!" shouted Iolaus.

Hercules wielded his sword like a scythe! Snake heads went flying through the air. Iolaus pressed the flaming stick against each neck, searing the flesh and stopping the heads growing back.

Pretty soon, there was only one chopped up Hydra and lots of dead heads.

"Wooh!" huffed Hercules. "That was tough!"

"Well, lets get back to the king," said Iolaus, jumping in the chariot.

"You take the chariot," said Hercules, climbing on top of one of the Hydra's heads. "I'll go on... *ahead!* BWAAHAHAHAAA!"

Hercules started laughing so hard he almost peed.

"That's terrible," groaned Iolaus.

"See cos we've got all these heads—"

"No, I get it," interrupted Iolaus. "It's just not funny."

"—and I'm on a head, like, I'm riding it. So when I said, 'I'll go on *ahead*' it's like, so funny, cos I'm actually ON A HEAD! HAAAAAAAAH!"

And Hercules kept laughing and laughing at his terrible joke, which just proves that even heroes can't be good at everything.

HERO SWAP CARDS

The Ancient Greek heroes were the original sports stars. Their stats were off the charts!
Swap 'em! Trade 'em! Collect the lot!

MASHED MYTHS! HERCULES

INTELLIGENCE	55
STRENGTH	99
TRICKINESS	50
FART POWER	Brutal

DID YOU KNOW?
Hercules was the strongest man ever – he once held up the sky for the god Atlas!

LIKES: Muscles, gyms, hairdressers, punching things.

DISLIKES: Sitting still, spelling tests, wearing undies.

DID YOU KNOW?

Theseus defeated the Minotaur, a terrifying monster that was half-man and half-bull

LIKES: Steak sandwiches, steak and fries, steak and eggs, steak and steak.

DISLIKES: Mazes, vegetables, dairy farms.

DID YOU KNOW?

Arachidamia was a queen of Sparta. She led the Spartans to a great victory over the Epirotes.

LIKES: Digging, trenches, gardening, shovels, holes, spades, pits, digging.

DISLIKES: Senators, Battle Elephants, Epirotes.

DID YOU KNOW?

Perseus killed Medusa, the evil Gorgon that could turn people to stone just by looking at them.

LIKES: Winged sandals, shiny shields, not being turned to stone.

DISLIKES: Snakes, snake hairdos, being turned to stone.

DID YOU KNOW?

Odysseus was super clever and super sneaky. He came up with the idea of the Trojan Horse.

LIKES: Horses, wood, wooden horses, crosswords, his wife.

DISLIKES: One-eyed giants, long sea journeys, island holidays.

Tale the Second
Perseus & Medusa
PART I

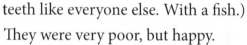

Perseus and his mother Danae lived in a fishing village on an island. All there was to do on the island was fish. So that's what everyone did. Fish. All day, every day. Fish, fish, fish. And because that's all anyone did, they ate loads of the stuff. Fish that is. Fish  breakfast. Fish lunch. Fish dinner. Fish pizza. Fish ice cream. Fish toothpaste. (That's probably not true because toothpaste hadn't been invented yet. Perseus brushed his teeth like everyone else. With a fish.) They were very poor, but happy.

Anyway, Perseus had just sat down for a hearty breakfast of FishFlakes™, when there was a knock on the door. It was the king of the island, Polydectes.

Now normally, a visit from a king is pretty cool. But for Perseus, it was definitely not cool at all.

See, King Polydectes wanted to marry Danae. Danae did not want to marry him, as the king was old, mean, and stank of fish. (Though to be fair, so did everyone on the island.)

Polydectes knew Perseus would try and stop the marriage, so he'd come up with a nasty plan to get rid of him. (See? Mean.)

The king decided that everyone on the island had to give him a present. If he didn't like your present, then you had to get him one he did like. (Rude!) So with this nasty plan in mind, he went and knocked loudly on Perseus's door.

KNOCK! KNOCK! KNOCK!

Perseus sighed and picked up the fish he had wrapped for the king's present.

"Is that a fish?" said the king, eyeing the present suspiciously.

"Maybe," replied Perseus.

"I don't want a fish," said the king.

"Maybe it's not a fish," said Perseus. "Maybe it's a horse."

"Oh. Is it a horse?"

"No, it's a fish."

"NO FISH!" roared the king. "I demand a new present! I demand… the head of a Gorgon!"

Gift Horse
(Do not look in mouth)

"Is that a fish?" Perseus asked hopefully.

"No!" shouted Polydectes with glee. "The Gorgons are three monstrous sisters that live near the setting sun. I want the head of their queen, Medusa! She has snakes for hair, and anyone who looks her in the eye is turned to stone!"

ONE GORGON HEAD
LOVE PERSEUS

Perseus peed his skirt a little bit. (Remember, Ancient Greece was proudly pants-free at this time.) Everyone knew of the terrifying monster Medusa. She was, well, terrifying!

"Off you go then," said the king with an evil grin. "And don't be too long, wouldn't want you to miss the wedding." He rode back to his palace, cackling nastily. Ha ha haaah, ah hah, hah, ha… Haaaaah… Hah.

Poor Perseus. He had no idea how to beat Medusa. He didn't even know where to find her. "Lives near the setting sun." What kind of address is that?!

The Gorgon Sisters
3 Setting Sun Way
Past the Horizon
Ancient Greece 71201

Suddenly, a clap of thunder shook the ground! In a PUFF of purple smoke stood a very, very beautiful man and woman.

"The Grey Sisters know how to find her," said the woman.

Perseus stared, openmouthed. The woman carried a shield of the brightest silver and a sword that crackled with bolts of lightning. The man wore sandals with little wings flapping on them. He hovered several inches above the ground.

"Gods!" thought Perseus. And he was right! Not just any gods either, but Hermes and Athena. Two of the best!

OLYMPUS LTD
Gods for every occasion!
ATHENA
Goddess of War
Do your war RIGHT!

YMPUS LTD
Gods for every occasion!
HERMES
Messenger of the Gods
Fast Delivery!
On time. Every time.

"First, wow," said Perseus. "Seriously, wow. And second, who are the Grey Sisters?"

"The Greys," said Athena in a voice like liquid music, "are three old hags."

"That's not very nice," said Perseus.

"Neither are they," replied Athena. "They're hideous and nasty. They share one eye between them. Only they know where Medusa lives, and they have sworn never to tell anyone. But I'm sure a clever lad like you can get it out of them."

"Okay, helpful. Sort of." said Perseus slowly. "But I've still got to defeat Medusa, and she's got this whole 'look at me and you'll turn to stone' thing going on. Plus, snakes for hair! Hello?!"

"These may help," said Athena, handing Perseus her sword and shield. The sword shone as he took it, and the shield flashed like a mirror.

"And these," said Hermes, kicking off his winged sandals.

"Remember," said Athena, "never look directly into Medusa's eyes, only into the reflection from the shield." *ZZINNG!* With a flash, Athena and Hermes were gone.

Perseus strapped on the sandals and streaked through the sky toward the home of the Grey Sisters. As he flew over the king's palace, he pooped on it for good measure.

"Bet they thought that was a mighty big pigeon," he grinned.

"Righto, all I've got to do now is trick the Grey Sisters, cut off Medusa's head, and get back in time to stop the creepy king marrying my mother."

It didn't sound so hard when he said it like that.

END OF PART I

BEASTS AND BADDIES

The Ancient Greeks believed in mythical monsters! Here are three of their craziest monsters...

CERBERUS

Cerberus was a giant three-headed dog that guarded the entrance of the Underworld. It had three heads, a serpent's tail, and loved chasing sticks.

THE HYDRA

The Hydra was a giant snake-like monster with nine heads, (must have taken ages for it to brush its teeth.) If one of the Hydra's heads was chopped off, two more would grow back!

THE CHIMERA

The Chimera was a monstrous fire-breathing creature that loved eating people. It was part lion, part goat, and part snake, and should have been called THE LIO-GOA-KE.

35

Perseus & Medusa
PART II

Perseus peered through the window of the grimy hut. Inside sat the Grey Sisters.

Hut
(Smellius Hovellus)

Empty eye sockets stared blindly from their shriveled heads. Dribble trickled down their toothless mouths.

One of them held up a single glistening eyeball. It stared down at whatever foul and hideous business lay upon the table. An evil smile spread across the sister's wrinkled face.

"What is it, Sister?" begged the two without the Eye. "What do you see?"

"I see… I see…" said the sister. "I see that the last piece goes here! Our jigsaw is complete! Ooh look it's a pussy cat! With a grumpy face! THAT'S SO CUTE!"

"I love jigsaw puzzles!" said the second sister.

"I really, really love cat jigsaw puzzles!" said the third.

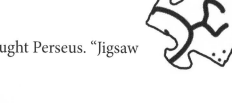

"Wait, what?" thought Perseus. "Jigsaw puzzles?"

"Let's do another!" shrieked the first sister.

"We haven't got any more! That was the last one." wailed the second.

"And that," thought Perseus, "is my chance."

He knocked on the front door, and in his best deliveryman voice announced, "Delivery! Cat jigsaw for the Gray Sisters!"

The three old hags almost fell over themselves as they scrambled to open the door. "A cat jigsaw for us!" they screamed. "Where is it?! Where is it?!"

"It's on the back of my chariot," said Perseus. "But I warn you, it's a big one. Fifteen thousand pieces! The box is huge. I hurt my back getting it here. So you'll have to carry it inside."

"Yes yes!" snapped the first sister. "Just show it to us!"

"Okay," said Perseus casually. "You want me to hold that slimy old eyeball while you get it?"

Mr. Cuddle Snuggles
1st Place
Cutest Cat Ever
Competition

"What? You want the Eye?" said the second sister suspiciously, clutching the eyeball tightly.

"Well, if you don't want this giant jigsaw puzzle of the cutest, fluffiest pussy cat you've ever seen, I can take it

back to the warehouse…"

"NO!!!!" squealed the other two sisters. "Cutest, fluffiest cat ever?! Just give him the Eye!"

"Fine," said the second sister, and she slapped the eyeball into Perseus's hand. Immediately he flew into the air on his winged sandals.

"Hahaaah! I have your Eye!" he yelled down at them.

"We've been tricked!" wailed one of the hags.

"Give it back! Now!" shrieked the other sisters.

"Now, now, ask nicely" Perseus said with a cheeky grin, tossing the eyeball up into the air and catching it, over and over again.

"Stop that! Please!" wailed one of the hags.

"It's making me dizzy!" moaned another. "I think I'm gunna puke!"

"I'll give it back, if you tell me where Medusa lives."

"What? No! We swore we'd never tell!"

Perseus spun the eyeball round and round and round.

"Oooh gawd. Yep, yep, I puked," said the youngest sister.

"Oops, I'm next," said the middle one.

"All right! Fine!" shrieked the eldest. "Just head towards the setting sun, then turn left. It's number 57 Gorgon Avenue, big abandoned temple, red mailbox. You can't miss it. NOW GIVE US THE EYE!!!"

"Thank you, ladies," said Perseus, dropping the eyeball to the ground. The hags scrabbled desperately in the dirt as Perseus flew off toward the setting sun.

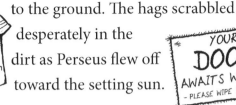

Finding the lair of Medusa wasn't hard (no one else nearby had a red mailbox). Perseus crept through the crumbling damp hallways. Broken stone statues stood everywhere, their faces twisted in terror.

SSSSsssssssss...

Snakes! Perseus froze. The hissing echoed off the walls. It seemed to come from everywhere at once! Perseus's heart beat so fast he felt it would explode. Trickles of sweat dribbled down his neck and into his butt crack.

Suddenly a large shadow slithered along the wall toward him. Perseus angled his shield up and stared at the Gorgon's reflection. A hideous monster stared back from the mirror-like surface. It had foul, hideous snakes for hair, skin like wet, moldy cheese, and fierce, glowing red eyes.

"Woah," thought Perseus. "And I thought I looked bad in the morning."

Medusa swung her head back and forth, sniffing the air. The snakes on her head hissed angrily. Someone was close! The Gorgon inched closer and closer to his hiding spot.

SNIFF-SNIFF

A rat scuttled in the darkness. Medusa hissed and turned towards the sound. This was his chance! Perseus flew out into the hallway. His magic sword *SWISSHHED* through the air. *SMASSHHH!* Her head crashed to the ground, landing at his feet, *PLOP.* The snakes hissed and writhed.

"Woot!" shrieked Perseus. "I've defeated Medusa!
Go Team Me!"

"You'll never get away with
thissss!" hissed the snakes.

"Aaagh! Talking snakes!" yelled Perseus. "Actually, that's
not the weirdest thing I've seen today." A low growl
rumbled through the temple.

"Oops," thought Perseus. "That's
right. Medusa has two sisters.
Time to go!"

Grabbing Medusa's head,
Perseus flew into the air and
raced back over the sea as fast as his winged
sandals would carry him. He had to stop that wedding!

The Gorgons
Setting Sun P.S.
4300 BCE

CRASH! Perseus landed smack in the middle of the throne
room. The king stood there in his wedding robes. Oh no!
Perseus was TOO LATE!

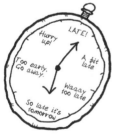

"Ah, you're just in time," snickered
Polydectes. "I was just about to marry
your mother."

"You haven't done it yet?" gasped Perseus.

"No, I had to change my wedding robes.
Got pooped on by what must have
been a massive pigeon. No matter,
you're too la—"

The king stopped midsentence, still as
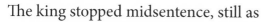
a stone statue—because he *was* a stone statue.
Perseus had held up the severed head of
Medusa. Even dead, her head still had the
power to turn people to stone.

The guests cheered wildly. They grabbed
Perseus and carried him around on their
shoulders and showered him with presents.
No one had liked Polydectes. No one. Not
even his parents. That's what a stinker he was.

Perseus and Danae put the
statue of the king out in
the square, where all the pigeons came
and pooped on it.

"Let's go home," said Perseus. "I'm dying
for a nice cold fish milkshake."

43

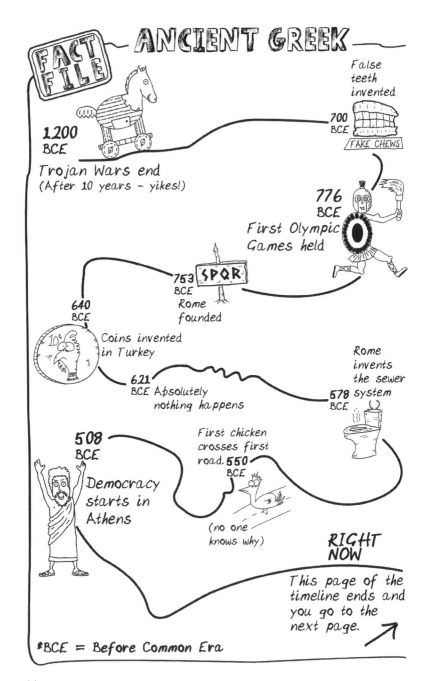

ANCIENT GREEK

FACT FILE

1200 BCE
Trojan Wars end
(After 10 years – yikes!)

700 BCE
False teeth invented
FAKE CHEWS

776 BCE
First Olympic Games held

753 BCE
Rome founded
SPQR

640 BCE
Coins invented in Turkey

621 BCE Absolutely nothing happens

578 BCE
Rome invents the sewer system

550 BCE
First chicken crosses first road.
(no one knows why)

508 BCE
Democracy starts in Athens

RIGHT NOW
This page of the timeline ends and you go to the next page.

*BCE = Before Common Era

TIME MACHINE

GREAT FARTS OF OUR TIME
by S. MELLY

180 BCE Books invented, yay!

146 BCE Rome conquers Greece

274 BCE Con the Average dies. No one cares

"MEH"

323 BCE Alexander the Great dies

362 BCE The car was not invented

400 BCE Persians invent ice cream (yum!)

POLICE BOX

432 BCE Parthenon built

480 BCE Battle of Thermopylae a.k.a. Battle of Salamis

@XP!!

Tale the Third
Theseus & the Minotaur
PART I

Theseus was the prince of Athens. That's a good thing right? Wrong! Athens at that time was beholden to (a fancy word that means "bossed around by") King Minos of Crete. Every year, the Athenians had to send fourteen girls and boys to Crete. Not for a holiday either (though Crete is very nice and you really should visit sometime). No. They were sent as sacrifices!

King Minos sent them into the Labyrinth: a maze of tunnels where he kept the fearsome monster, the Minotaur.

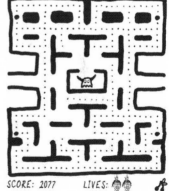

SCORE: 2077   LIVES:

"This has to stop!" Theseus shouted at his father (who was a bit deaf, Theseus wasn't just being rude). "I am determined to slay this beast."

"Slay the Minotaur!" the king shouted back (Theseus was also a bit deaf. It ran in the family). "Impossible! It's half man! Half bull! All terrifying! Razor-sharp horns! Glowing red eyes! No one ever has escaped the Labyrinth. No one! How about a nice beach holiday instead?"

Greetings from Sunny
CRETE!
Wish You Were Here!
(instead of me)

"No, father," declared Theseus. "These sacrifices must stop! Plus I don't like the beach. I always get sand in my toga. No, I shall slay the Minotaur and free our people."

So on a gloomy, windy day, Theseus and the thirteen other sacrifices sailed for Crete.

It was all very well to say he was going to defeat the Minotaur, but the only problem was, Theseus didn't know how. According to Greekopedia™, the Labyrinth was impossible to escape. Even if he killed the creature, how was he going to find his way out?

NO WAY OUT
NOT THIS WAY
NOPE!
UH-UH
WRONG

Theseus stared glumly out over the choppy gray waves.

"I'm scared," said a small voice beside him.
Theseus looked down at a small boy
clutching the rail of the ship.

"Hello, Scared," said Theseus. "I'm
Theseus."

"No, I'm not 'Scared'," said the boy. "I mean, I am scared.
Seriously, I've wet my toga twice. My name's
Little Jimmy. And I'm very frightened."

"Never fear Little Jimmy," replied Theseus
with a confidence he didn't really feel. "I
won't let anything happen to you."

"Aw, thanks, Theseus," said Little Jimmy
happily. "That makes me feel way better. I
better go and change my toga, again."

As he turned back to watch the
waves, Theseus realized he was a bit
scared himself.

"I should have packed another
toga," he thought with a shiver.

TOGA
WASHING
INSTRUCTIONS
Do Not
Tumble Dry!
(Because tumble
dryers haven't been
invented yet, duh.)

Finally, they docked at Crete. The walls of the city were packed with people eager to see the latest sacrifices from Athens. As Theseus walked down the gangplank, he was amazed at how beautiful Crete was. (See? Told you.) But even more lovely than the island was the woman standing on the wharf.

She was more beautiful than two scoops of hokey pokey ice cream on a hot summer's day. She smelled better than a pair of freshly ironed undies, and when she smiled, his heart skipped a beat.

He smoothed back his hair, puffed out his chest, and smiled his best princely smile.

"Hi," said Theseus. "I'm Theseus. And when I saw you, my heart skipped a beat."

"You should probably see a doctor then," said the girl. "That sounds like a serious medical condition. I am Princess Ariadne, daughter of King Minos."

"A princess!" thought Theseus. "Wow!"

A huge hairy arm suddenly wrapped around his shoulders. The arm belonged to the huge hairy King Minos.

"Howdy!" the king's gruff voice roared in his ear. "You must be Theseus. What can I get you?"

"Ummm, a date with Ariadne?" said Theseus.

The king roared with laughter. "You're funny! Funny guy. But I'm sorry, she doesn't date food. And you'll be a Minotaur's dinner by tomorrow!"

"What if I defeat the Minotaur?" Theseus snapped back at him.

The king laughed even harder. "You crack me up, Theseus. I'd say you should do live comedy, but you'll be dead soon. I tell you what, if you can defeat the Minotaur and escape the Labyrinth, you can marry my daughter. BWAHAHAAAAH! In the meantime, it's off to the dungeon for you!"

And with that, the guards grabbed Theseus, Little Jimmy, and the others and dragged them away.

END OF PART I

COW AMAZIN' IS THAT?

Build Your Own Ancient Greek Maze
in Three Simple Steps!

Building a maze is really easy.

1. Get your building material. This can be anything from Lego to underpants. Then build your maze.

2. Once your maze is made, put a really deadly magical creature like a Hydra, Minotaur, or Chimera in the maze.

3. Now put any of your family in it and see if they can escape without being eaten.

See? Simple!

Theseus & the Minotaur
PART II

Theseus paced around the dungeon. Tomorrow he was to be sent into the Labyrinth to be eaten by the Minotaur. He needed a plan.

"I need a plan," said Theseus.

— Hairless Rick's —
CUNNING PLANS!
For Every Occasion!
·Escape plans · Wedding plans · Escape from Wedding plans·

"What about my invisibility potion?" said Little Jimmy.

NOTHING 2 SEE HERE
Invisibility Potion
If your friends could see you now!

"That's fantastic!" exclaimed Theseus. "Where is it?"

"I can't find it," replied Little Jimmy. "It's invisible."

"So close!" sighed Theseus, "Okay, another plan then. Hmmm... What do bulls like?"

"Ummm, cows?" said Little Jimmy.

"Yes! What else?"

"Grass?"

"Definitely! This is good stuff, Jimmy! What else?"

"Errr, music?"

"Brilliant! That's it! I've got a plan! A brilliant, brilliant, brilliant plan!"

"What is it?" asked Little Jimmy excitedly.

"I'll dress up as a cow, offer the Minotaur some grass, and then smash it over the head with a guitar!"

"Theseus, you are a genius," said Little Jimmy. "How many of those things have we got?"

"None."

"Did you count them?"

"Twice."

Little Jimmy shook his head sadly. "I guess we're just going to get eaten by the Minotaur then," he said.

"Pssssst!" came a sound.

"Do you need to change your toga again?" asked Theseus.

"That wasn't me!" snapped Little Jimmy. "It came from the window."

Theseus ran over and peered through the bars. Outside, lit by the glowing light of a lamp, was the beautiful Ariadne, the king's daughter.

"I've come to save you!" she whispered.

"Fantastic!" exclaimed Theseus. "Do you have a cow suit, some grass, and a guitar?"

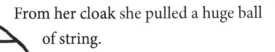

"Errr, no," said Ariadne. "But what I have got is this."

From her cloak she pulled a huge ball of string.

"Great, thanks," said Theseus. "I've always wanted a giant ball of string. That would be really useful. IF I WAS A CAT!"

Ariadne sighed. She liked Theseus a lot. She just wished he wasn't so dumb.

"So you don't get lost in the maze," she said slowly, "tie one end of the string to the door, then roll it out in front of you. When you've defeated the beast, follow it

silly string

back to the entrance so you don't get lost."

"Ohhhh, right," said Theseus, "Got it. Sorry about the cat thing. Now, do you have a guitar?"

sensible string

"I've got something better," Ariadne said with a grin.

"A ukulele?"

"What? No," said Ariadne. "I've brought you a sword."

Moo-kulele

"Oh," said Theseus. "I was hoping it would be a ukulele."

"Just take the sword!" said Little Jimmy.

There was a jangle of keys in the dungeon door. The guards! They'd come to take the sacrifices off to the Labyrinth. Ariadne clutched Theseus's hand.

"All I ask for helping you," she said, "is that you'll marry me and take me away from this cruel place." She stood on tiptoe, planted a kiss on Theseus's lips, and  disappeared into the dark.

"Woah!" gasped Theseus.

"Gross," muttered Little Jimmy.

THE NEXT MORNING...

Theseus stood before the huge Labyrinth door.

"Righto," said King Minos. "Off you go. I'd say 'see you soon', but we both know that's not going to happen."

Laughing nastily, the guards shoved Theseus into the dark corridor. The door CLANGED shut behind him. He tied the string to the door handle and slipped into the gloom.

The Labyrinth was huge. Corridors branched off everywhere. Orange torchlight flickered against the stone walls, making everything look the same. Within moments, Theseus was completely lost. Only the string back to the front door kept him from panicking.

58

A low "Mooo!" echoed through the corridors. It seemed to come from everywhere at once! Terrified, Theseus crept forward, his feet crunching on old bones. A terrible smell hit his nostrils.

 "Is that me?" thought Theseus, "I knew I should have washed my socks."

"MOOOOO!" Theseus whirled around! The ball of string tumbled from his trembling hands. It rolled across the floor and stopped between the two massive hooves of THE MINOTAUR!

THE MINOTAUR! Eight feet tall, bulging muscles, and the hideous head of a giant bull. Fiery steam snorted from its nostrils and its eyes glowed red in the gloomy light.

59

"TremBULL before me, puny human!" roared the Minotaur "For I am in a terrible MOOOOOOO-D!"

"Please don't kill m—wait, what?" said Theseus. "Are you making awful cow puns?"

"BULL!" roared the Minotaur.

"There's no need to swear," said Theseus

"No! They're BULL puns. Not cow puns," thundered the beast. "And they're not awful."

"Eh," said Theseus, making a face.

"Everyone's a critic," snapped the Minotaur. "Doesn't matter, I'm going to have you for breakfast!"

He put his mighty head down and charged towards Theseus.

"You'll have me for breakfast?" said Theseus as he dodged the Minotaur's lunging horns. "I thought you would have had MOO-sli!"

Stop with the jokes!" raged the monster. "They're terrible!"

Suddenly, the ball of string tangled around one of his hooves. DING! A light bulb went off in Theseus's head. (Which is definitely how the light bulb got invented.)*

*Not really

Theseus kicked the ball of string so it wrapped around the Minotaur's other leg.

"Don't you mean terriBULL?" asked Theseus, ducking under smashing hooves. He flicked the ball of string once more around the beast's ankles. "You sure you don't want to hear an-UDDER one?"

"You are so dead!" screamed the Minotaur.

"Last one, I promise," said Theseus. "What do you call a bull with no legs?"

"Ummm… I don't know," said the Minotaur.

"Ground beef!" And with that, Theseus heaved on the ball of string. The Minotaur's legs were pulled from underneath it! With an ear shattering "MOOOOOOO!" it crashed to the ground! Theseus raced forward and plunged his sword into the monster.

"I'm going to put you in a MOO-seum!" said Theseus.

"Please… no more… bad jokes." gasped the Minotaur with its final breath, then died.

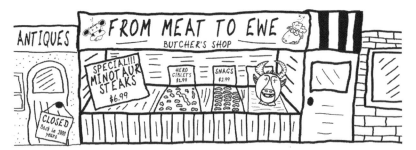

Theseus dusted himself off and followed the string back to the maze entrance.

As he walked out of the Labyrinth, King Minos's jaw dropped in astonishment! But Ariadne, Little Jimmy, and the other Athenians jumped and cheered for joy.

"Theseus!" gasped Ariadne. "You did it! You defeated the Minotaur! We can get married! I am so happy!"

"Yes" said Theseus with a grin. "It's all so very MOO-ving."

Ariadne stopped smiling.

"Ummm, I think I've changed my mind."

MONSTER MASH

Ever thought you might be an Ancient Greek monster?
Yes? Then this quiz is for you!

INSTRUCTIONS:

Add up the points from your answers to see if you're an
ANCIENT GREEK MONSTER!

---

1. What would you like to be when you grow up?

(a) Guardian of the Golden Fleece (6 points)

(d) Bus driver (2 points)

(c) Half human and half bull (8 points)

(d) Dog washer (4 points)

2. Your favorite snack is:

(a) Ancient Greek heroes (8 points)

(b) Ice cream (4 points)

(c) Anything that moves (6 points)

(d) Pizza (2 points)

3. Your special monster power would be:

(a) Turning people into stone (8 points)

(b) Never forgetting your lunch box (2 points)

(c) Shooting fire from your mouth (6 points)

(d) Knowing your nine times table
(4 points)

To see if you are an Ancient Greek monster, add up your score!

6 – 12 points   You're a big fluffy
unicorn cloud.

13 – 17 You'd definitely win first prize
on Halloween.

18 – 24 Total Monster! Take your
pick: Medusa, Cerberus, any of them.
You're a major monster!

Tale the Fourth
Arachidamia & the Epirotes
PART I

Arachidamia was queen of Sparta. Being a queen is pretty awesome. You can eat ice cream for dinner, wear your pajamas all day, ride your horse in your bedroom, or all three at once if you want. It's good to be the queen.

However, what Arachidamia loved most of all was digging in her garden. She dug holes, channels, trenches, ditches, cavities, hollows, craters, potholes, pits–you name it, she dug it.

Her garden shed was filled with a huge collection of shovels, trowels, spades, and even spoons (for very small holes, and sometimes ice cream).

Frog Mouth
Ice Cream Hoe

Some people thought Arachidamia liked digging so much because she came from a long line of pirates who loved burying treasure. Others said it was because her father was a god and her mother was a badger (Don't ask. It's an Ancient Greek thing). But the truth was that Arachidamia loved digging because it relaxed her, and being a queen, she didn't often get time to relax. Queens are busy.

One particularly busy morning, after Arachidamia had already waved to her subjects from the palace balcony, passed six new laws, opened a supermarket and judged eleven court cases, her chambermaid Missy burst in, followed by a bunch of frantic maids.

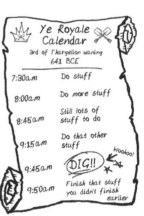

Ye Royale Calendar
3rd of Thargelion waning
641 BCE

7:30a.m	Do stuff
8:00a.m	Do more stuff
8:45a.m	Still lots of stuff to do
9:15a.m	Do that other stuff
9:45a.m	DIG!! Woohoo!
9:50a.m	Finish that stuff you didn't finish earlier

"Your Majesty!" gasped Missy. "The Epirotes are coming!"

"Well, I was just going to do a spot of digging." Arachidamia sighed. "Tell Cook to put some scones on for them, and I'll be up later."

QUEEN DIGGING

Needle Nose
Sod Scooper

68

"No," said Missy. "The Epirote army! They've come to attack us! The Spartan Senate has said that all women and children must leave the city for their safety!"

"Evacuate?!" shouted the queen "I've got digging to do! I've got a hole going in the southeast corner that I'm going to turn into a pit. I'm not leaving!"

Flat Pan
Gravel Flicker

She slung her shovel over her shoulder and stormed off to the Great Hall of the Senate.

We're doomed!!!   Help!!   Surrender Now!

Run away!   Knock Knock!

Who wants sandwiches?!?

SENATE

The senators were in a state of uproar when Arachidamia and her large crowd of women arrived. The old men that made up the Senate were wheezing and blathering as if their lives depended on it. Which in this case, they did.

Blather - Bottom   ∴ DICTIONARY

Blather:(blaTHar) To talk lots, like heaps and heaps without making any sense and just keep going on and on and and on and ON AND ON AND I'M SO BORED! HE'S STILL TALKING! SOMEBODY MAKE HIM SHUT UP PLEASE!!!!!!!!!!!!!

"Our armies are away fighting the Cretans!" gurgled Gastronomos, a huge, blubbery Senator. "There is no one to defend us! Also, it's nearly lunch time."

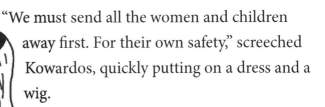

"We're doomed!" wailed Senator Kowardos. "I vote we surrender immediately!"

"After lunch, though," replied Gastronomos, munching on a giant turkey leg.

"We must send all the women and children away first. For their own safety," screeched Kowardos, quickly putting on a dress and a wig.

CLANG!!! Arachidamia slammed her shovel down. The room went silent.

"We're not leaving!" she announced loudly. "The women of Sparta shall stay and defend our city and its people!"

Splay-footed
Chunk Chucker

"With all due respect, Your Majesty," mumbled Gastronomos through a mouthful of turkey. "We are the wise old men of Sparta. We know what's best for you ladies."

He smiled and patted Arachidamia on the head "Now run along like a good gir—" SCHTONGGGGGG!!!

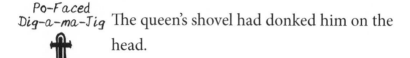

Po-Faced Dig-a-ma-Jig The queen's shovel had donked him on the head.

"Sorry," said Arachidamia with a sweet smile. "Must have slipped."

She strode into the center of the chamber and fixed each trembling old Senator with a fiercesome glare.

"Honestly!" she said. "You men are all acting like a herd of frightened sheep!"

"Oh, do sheep get to leave too?" said Kowardos, quickly throwing a lambskin over his head.

"We are Spartans!" roared Arachidamia. "We do not run! We shall fight the Epirotes to the last woman!"

These Spartans Don't Run

71

"But what about the Epirote Battle Elephants?" whined Kowardos. "Maybe we could beat the regular soldiers. Even regular elephants. But Battle Elephants?"

Regular Elephant

"Spartan women can defeat anything!" the queen exclaimed.

"You all agree, then?" demanded Gastronomos grumpily, nursing the shovel-shaped bruise on his head. "You want to stay here and die a gruesome, grisly death at the hands (or tusks) of the savage Epirote army?"

BATTLE ELEPHANT!

"YES!" chorused the women loudly.

"We will not only fight them," said Arachidamia proudly, "we will beat them".

"How?" Gastronomos sneered.

Arachidamia grinned, and lifted her shovel high.

"Women of Sparta," she commanded, "to the garden shed!"

END OF PART I

SPARTAN SCHOOL DAZE

The Spartans lived in southern Greece. They had one of the best armies EVER. They were so tough that even today the word 'Spartan' means sparse and brave.

FACT FILE

To test for strength Spartan babies were left out on a hill, where only the strongest survived.

What do you call a group of baby soldiers?

INFANTRY!

Boys left their families when they were seven and trained for twenty-three years to become soldiers.

SPARTA HIGH

Alright children, who wants to fight the monster first?

Spartan soldiers were expected to fight without fear and never ever, ever, EVER give up!

Arachidamia & the Epirotes
PART II

King Pyrrhus was very excited. Super excited. He was so excited he could hardly stand still.

"Isn't this exciting?!" he exclaimed, excitedly, to his top general, Colin.

"Very exciting, sire" replied Colin. "We shall finally defeat the Spartans and take their city."

"What? No!" said Pyrrhus. "The Olympics are about to start! THE OLYMPICS! I love the Olympics!"

"Right. Ah… Shouldn't we be thinking about the battle, sire?" said Colin.

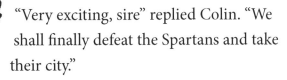

"Battle schmattle!" shouted Pyrrhus. "The Olympics starts in THREE DAYS! There's people running and chucking stuff and jumping over things and shouting a lot."*

Battle	Olympics
☑ running	☑ running
☑ chucking stuff	☑ chucking stuff
☑ shouting	☑ shouting
☑ dying	☑ dying
☑ pointless	☑ pointless

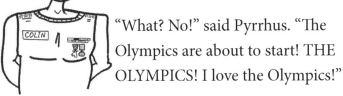

*Want to know about the Ancient Olympics? Turn to page 86!

"That pretty much describes a battle, sire."

"But they're doing it to win pretty wreaths for
their heads, so it's different. Let's get this
battle done with. I've got tickets to
the diving. ATTACK!!!!"

The general sighed. "We can't just
attack, sire. We have to consult the soothsayer. He'll tell us
if the gods think it's a good day to go to war."

"You're such a downer, Colin," moaned Pyrrhus. "Fine.
Bring him in. I don't really see the
point, though. I've got Battle
Elephants."

A small hairy man, covered in
stinky furs, entered the tent. He
closed his eyes, and
then picked his nose with one dirty finger.

"Gross," muttered Pyrrhus. "What's he
doing?"

"Looking for a sign from the gods, sire."

"Up his nose?" said Pyrrhus incredulously. "What god lives up there? Boogerus?"

The soothsayer suddenly SCREECHED! He plucked an enormous booger from his nostril. He studied it intently for a minute, then ate it.

"Yeah, nah," said the Soothsayer. "No good. No war today." And with that, he scuttled out of the tent.

Mon	Tue	Wed	Thu	Fri
Good day for war ①	*Don't do war today! Bad day for war ②	Good day for some war (stop by 1p.m.) ③	Good day for fishing! (Check with Poseidon first) ④	Bad day for war (Dinner at mom's) ⑤

"Do I pay him?" said King Pyrrhus. "Seriously? Am I paying for that?"

The general shrugged helplessly. "I'm sure we can attack tomorrow, sire".

MEANWHILE, BACK IN SPARTA...

Queen Arachidamia had gathered all the women into her garden. (It was a very big garden. She was queen after all.)

"My loyal subjects," said Arachidamia, "to win we need to beat those Battle Elephants. Luckily, I have a cunning plan. What don't elephants like?"

Answers came flying back from the crowd thick and fast.

"Rhinoceroses!"

"Sunglasses!"

"Rhinoceroses wearing sunglasses!"

"Wearing undies!"

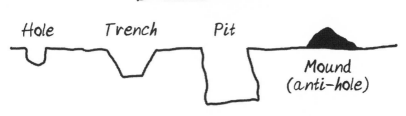

The queen raised her hand for silence.

"All good answers", she said. "But what I was thinking was, holes."

HOLE-APEDIA

Hole   Trench   Pit

Mound
(anti-hole)

"How do you 'think' a hole?" said Missy. "Normally, you'd dig one."

"Exactly!" exclaimed Arachidamia. "You do dig holes. Big holes! Elephants have stumpy legs, so they can't step over things easily. Get what I mean?"

Is that a thinkhole?

Yeth!

"Totally," said Missy. "Except for the bit about the holes. And the legs. And the elephants. Apart from that, I'm all over it."

Arachidamia smiled. "We'll dig a deep, wide trench all around the city," she said. "When the elephants reach the trench, they will stop in terror, throw their riders off, and run away, trampling the army behind them."

Elephant
(stumpy leg)

"That's brilliant, Your Majesty!" exclaimed Missy.

Horse
(Not stumpy leg)

"I know," said Arachidamia. "I'm a queen, it's what I do. Be brilliant."

"Except," said Missy, "digging a trench that big would take hundreds of people! And hundreds of shovels!"

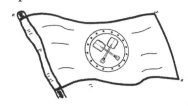

Arachidamia threw open the doors to her garden shed. Inside glittered her huge collection of shovels, spades, trowels, scoops, and spoons.

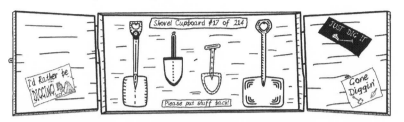

"Then," said Arachidamia with a determined look, "we better get started."

THE NEXT MORNING...

King Pyrrhus's breakfast was covered in dust. So was his tent. So was the entire Epirote camp.

"Is this normal?" Pyrrhus asked General Colin. "It's just I'm not usually up this early."

"Ah, no, sire," coughed the General. "All this dust seems to be coming from the city of Sparta."

"Perhaps they're all running away?" said Pyrrhus. "That'll make for a quicker battle. Excellent! ATTACK!"

General Colin raised his eyebrows at the king.

"What?" said Pyrrhus. "Oh right, the soothsayer. That is such a pain."

Just then, a very dusty messenger raced up to the king and handed him a very dusty message. Pyrrhus's eyes widened in shock.

"What is it, sire?" asked the general urgently. "Have the Spartan armies returned to fight us? Has the great land of Epirus been struck by plague?"

"It's worse than that," moaned the King. "THE OLYMPICS HAVE BEEN MOVED FORWARD BY A DAY! If I don't get this battle done right now, I'll miss the opening ceremony!"

Just then the soothsayer arrived, his finger already moving toward his nostril. Pyrrhus leapt up and grabbed him by the collar.

"Now listen, Stinky McFuture," hissed the king. "This can go two ways. Either you say this is a good day for war and you live a long and stinky life, or you say this is a bad day for war and I find myself a new soothsayer who is less dead than you. What's it going to be?"

"Ummmm," gulped the soothsayer. "Let me check my booger. Oh wow, look at that. This booger says, 'Best day for war ever!'"

Booger says yes.

"That's one wise booger," said Pyrrhus with a nasty grin. "Ready the Battle Elephants! ATTACK!"

MEANWHILE, OUTSIDE THE CITY OF SPARTA...

BOOM! BOOM! BOOM! The ground trembled like an earthquake. The Battle Elephants were coming!

81

The beasts were enormous: three stories high, covered with spiked armor, and carrying almost the entire Epirote army on their backs. The

Eh, I've seen bigger.

mighty creatures trumpeted their war cries as they charged towards the city.

Behind the wide, deep trench now surrounding the city, Arachidamia and her women warriors stood ready. The queen wore gleaming battle armor, and carried her favorite shovel.

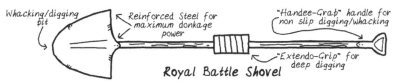

Whacking/digging bit

← Reinforced Steel for maximum donkage power

"Handee-Grab" handle for non slip digging/whacking

"Extendo-Grip" for deep digging

Royal Battle Shovel

"Steady, ladies," she muttered as the gigantic monsters thundered toward them.

"They're huge!" squeaked Missy. "Are you sure this is going to work?"

"Ask me afterward" replied Arachidamia grimly. "Shovels at the ready!"

The women of Sparta snapped their spades, trowels, and spoons into fighting positions. The earth shuddered as the Battle Elephants pounded closer.

The first beast was almost upon them! It reared up, legs like tree trunks ready to stomp down and squash the women to a pulp!

BAWAAARRRRGH!!! The mighty creature suddenly skidded to a halt at the lip of the trench, eyes wild with fear! The trench! It couldn't cross the trench! The soldiers on its back went crashing to the ground.

Urrk!

SCREEEEECH!!!

Another Battle Elephant suddenly SLAMMED into the back of the first elephant. More soldiers fell and got squashed as all the Battle Elephants panicked and ran around out of control. Trumpeting loudly, the elephants stampeded back toward the Epirote camp.

"That's it!" shrieked Arachidamia, "Time to finish them! CHAAAARRRRGGGE!!!"

The women raced forward into the battle, *Eeep!* thwacking and smacking the remaining soldiers with their shovels and spades.

BACK IN THE EPIROTES CAMP...

King Pyrrhus stared across the plain at the approaching elephants.

"Are those our elephants?" he said to the general.

"Yes, sire," replied the general.

Eeep!

"Are they supposed to be running back toward us?"

Booger says No.

"No, sire."

"I'm not going to make it to the Olympics, am I?"

"Unlikely, sire"

All welcome! (No minotaurs)
OLYMPIC TICKETS FOR SALE
Unable to use due to unexpected squashing by elephant. (tickets are now a bit flat but should still be good.)
250 Drachmas OBO.

FOR SALE: TROJAN HORSE.
Used once! Great for tricking

"Poo," said King Pyrrhus, and was promptly squashed by a rampaging Battle Elephant.

FINALLY, BACK IN SPARTA...

Dusty, sore, but happy, the women of Sparta carried Arachidamia through the city.

"VICTORY!" they chanted. "HOORAY FOR QUEEN ARACHIDAMIA!"

The queen smiled. "Just drop me off at my shed."

"But aren't you coming to the victory party?" asked Missy.

"I'll be up later," replied Arachidamia, "but first I've got a spot of digging to do."

ANCIENT WORLD
THE OLYMPICS

The Greeks started the Olympic Games over 2,700 years ago in Olympia, in southern Greece.

OLYMPIA
TIDY TOWN 750 BCE

The most popular race was the egg and spoon race.*

*Possibly not true.

Ancient Olympic athletes competed in the NUDE!!!

There were no gold, silver, and bronze medals. Winners were given a wreath of leaves and a hero's welcome back home.

The very first winner of the Olympic Games was a baker called Coroebus of Elis. (Some people say he was half-baked.)

OF SPORTS!
THE HERAEANS

WOMEN ONLY

Married women were not allowed to go to the Olympics, so they started their own games.

The games were called the Heraean Games after the goddess Hera (who was Zeus's wife).

Unlike the men in the Olympics, the women in the Heraeans could wear clothes.

The most popular event was the sack race.*

*Also possibly not true.

The woman who won the most races was called the Grand Heraean and got a new hairdo.* After all, it was called the HAIR-aean games!

*Possibly certainly not true.

Tale the Fifth
Odysseus & the Cyclops
PART I

Odysseus was a smart guy. How smart? Well, think of the two smartest people you know. Then add them together twice, and you would have someone almost as smart as Odysseus. That's how smart he was. He would have been called Odysseus the Smarty Pants, except that pants hadn't been invented and Odysseus the Smarty Who Doesn't Wear Pants sounds a bit weird.

Odysseus's brain

Your brain

He was always thinking of clever stuff like "How to beat the Trojans during the Siege of **Troy?**"* (use a wooden horse!) or "How to pick dirty socks up off the floor without bending down?" (just don't pick them up!)

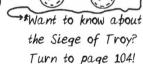

→*Want to know about the Siege of Troy? Turn to page 104!

Like I said, smart with a capital SMART. But as he looked up at the huge one-eyed giant that was currently munching down on two of his sailors, he wasn't sure if he was smart enough to get out of this one.

To be fair, it wasn't his fault that he and his entire crew were trapped in a cave inhabited by a vicious Cyclops (previously mentioned one-eyed giant) whose favorite food was smelly sailors.

He had been sailing back from Troy after beating the Trojans with his wooden

horse, and was eager to get back to his wife, Penelope. But his crew was hungry and tired, so when they passed a beautiful looking island, they begged him to stop.

"Come on," whined Barry the First Mate. "We've been on this boat forever. I wanna stop."

Odysseus wasn't so sure. There was something about this place that didn't feel right.

Maybe it was the dark, gloomy clouds that hung over the island. Maybe it was the way the wind whispered, "You're all going to die!" The huge pile of human skulls on the beach really should have been a dead giveaway.

DANGER!
CYCLOPS AHEAD
Drive Slowly

Nevertheless, Odysseus looked at his exhausted crew and made one of his not so smart decisions. (Even really smart people do that sometimes.)

"All right." He sighed. "But just for a minute and stay on the beach." Too late! His crew leapt off the boat and scrambled up a grassy hill.

"Oh well," thought Odysseus. "What's the worst that could happen?"*

GOOD   BAD   WORSE

(*You should never ever say "What's the worst that could happen?" as it's guaranteed to make the worst that could happen, happen. Odysseus really should have known better, but as I said, he was having an off day.)

Odysseus followed his crew up the hills towards a large cave. Barry the First Mate suddenly came rushing up, chewing on a huge roast leg of lamb.

91

"Ohdymth! Hoo hot oo ee imph! Hohal hahoh!!!"

"What?"

Barry pulled the leg of lamb out of his mouth. "Sorry. Odysseus! You've got to see this! Total jackpot!" He rushed back inside the cave.

It was a total jackpot indeed. Inside, the cave was filled with food and drink! Juicy smoked turkeys hung from the ceiling. Hundreds of freshly cooked sizzling sausages were piled up on plates next to massive barrels of wine, and crates of delicious olives were stacked to the roof!

Odysseus looked around cautiously as his crew stuffed their faces. There really was a lot of food. Enough food for a hundred people. Or just one really, really big person.

"Ummmm. I'm not sure this is a good idea, guys," murmured Odysseus.

"Come on, Oddy," gurgled Barry through mouthfuls of food, "what's the worst thing that could happen?"

Just then, the worst thing that could happen, happened.*

The cave suddenly darkened. A gigantic figure, two stories tall and dressed in stinking furs, blocked the entrance. Its enormous feet were like boats and smelled worse than a wet dog's armpit! One massive bloodshot eye, right in the middle of its greasy forehead, glared down at the sailors.

*See?! Told you.

BOAT SHOES

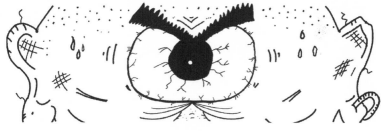

A herd of nervous sheep mingled around its tree-like legs and bleated at the crew.

Barry stared back in horror, mid-chew.

"Pssst, Oddy," whispered Barry. "I think it might be time to go."

The Cyclops licked its lips with a slimy, leathery tongue. It grinned down at the terrified sailors. A thunderous voice rumbled from its throat.

93

"My favorite snack, smelly sailors. Oh, I do love smelly sailors," he chuckled.

Quick as lightning, the giant snatched up two of the crew and stuffed them into his gaping mouth. Two quick CHOMPS and a GULP and the men were gone.

Odysseus gasped in terror! Barry threw up a little bit on the floor!

"Mmmm", said the giant, "Smelly AND Salty."

The monster brought his sheep inside the cave. Then with a huge HEAVE of his mighty arms, rolled a massive stone across the entrance. Odysseus and his crew were trapped.

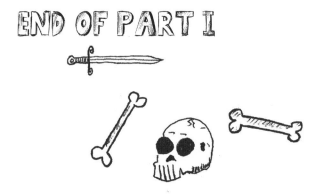

END OF PART I

GREEK ALPHABET SOUP

Did you know the word "alphabet" comes from the Greek letters "Alpha" & "Beta"? The Greek Alphabet is over 2750 years old! Try writing your name in Ancient Greek.

MASHED MYTHS looks like this:

ΜΑΣΗΕΔ ΜΨΤΗΣ

A — A — ALPHA	**B** — B — BETA	**C** — χ — CHI	**D** — Δ — DELTA
E — E — EPSILON	**F** — Φ — PHI	**G** — Γ — GAMMA	**H** — H — ETA
I — I — IOTA	**K** — K — KAPPA	**L** — Λ — LAMBDA	**M** — M — MU
N — N — NU	**O** — O — OMICRON	**P** — Π — PI	**Q** — Θ — THETA
R — P — RHO	**S** — Σ — SIGMA	**T** — T — TAU	**U** — Y — UPSILON
W — Ω — OMEGA	**X** — Ξ — XI	**Y** — Ψ — PSI	**Z** — Z — ZETA

Odysseus & the Cyclops
PART II

Odysseus and his crew huddled in a corner, terrified. The Cyclops had eaten two more sailors and was now sitting by the fire, guzzling wine and picking its teeth with a massive toothpick the size of a tree.

Ethan   Barry   Odysseus

But Odysseus wasn't super smart for nothing. As he watched the giant and his one big eye, a cunning plan began to form in his clever mind.

"Stay close to the sheep," he muttered to his sailors.

"Way ahead of you!" Barry's muffled voice came from underneath one of the woolly animals, "I've called this one *Baarbra.*"

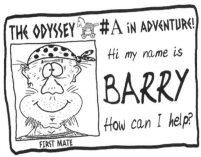

Odysseus put on his bravest voice and yelled over to the giant.

"Excuse me, but you've got a bit of sailor caught in your teeth".

"Oh, have I?" rumbled the Cyclops. He flicked a piece of half-chewed foot out of his gums with the massive toothpick. "How embarrassing! Thanks. Just for that, I'll eat you last then. What's your name, so I know?"

"Uhhh… Nobody," said Odysseus.

"Hey," said Barry, "that's not your name—oof!" ("Oof" is the official sound you make when someone elbows you hard in the stomach to stop you from giving away a brilliant plan.)

"Hello, Nobody." The giant burped. "I'm Polyphemus. Pleased to EAT you. BWAAAHAHAHAAAA!"

"Yes, very funny," replied Odysseus. "I couldn't help notice that you have a lot of wine."

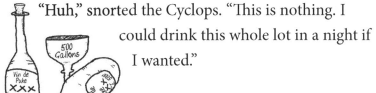

"Huh," snorted the Cyclops. "This is nothing. I could drink this whole lot in a night if I wanted."

"Really? No way!" exclaimed Odysseus. "No one could drink that much!"

"Are you calling me a liar?!" roared Polyphemus.

"No no no no no!" said Odysseus very quickly. "It's just seems very hard to do."

"Watch me!" Polyphemus snapped back. He jumped up and guzzled down three enormous barrels of wine one after another.

"Shee?" the giant slurred, "And itsh got no effect whatshoevrr." He let out a huge belch.

BURRRRPP!

Then another...

BUURRRRRRPP!!!

Then....

SMASHHH!!!

Polyphemus crashed to the floor, snoring loudly.

Quickly, Odysseus called his crew over and explained the rest of his plan.

"Right, so everybody got that? Good. Wait. Who's that?"

One of the sailors looked a bit… woolly.

"New crew member," said Barry. "I figured we needed replacements."

"Barry, is that a sheep?" said Odysseus

"No! Maybe. Yes," said Barry, sheepishly. "It's Baarbra."

Odysseus looked at the sheep in the sailor's outfit, then shrugged. If anything, Baarbra seemed a bit smarter than Barry.

Odysseus's
brain

Your
brain

Barry's
brain

"All right" said Odysseus. "Let's do this!"

The sailors heaved the giant toothpick onto their shoulders. It was sharp. Very sharp.

Pointy End

Not Pointy End

"One. Two. Three. Go!"

With a yell, they ran forward and rammed the giant toothpick into the Cyclops's eye!

The giant was blind! He screamed in pain!

"I'LL KILL YOU!" the Cyclops bellowed.

"Not if you can't see me!" Odysseus chuckled.

BOOM! BOOM! BOOM!

There was a loud knock on the massive stone that blocked the cave entrance. The other Cyclops on the island had come to find out what all the racket was about.

"Polyphemus! What's going on in there? Who's in there?!" the giants called.

"Nobody's in here!" roared the Cyclops, "Nobody!"

"What?" said the other giants, "Have you been on the wine again?"

"No! I mean, yes! But that's not the problem! Nobody attacked me! Nobody hurt me!"

The other giants roared with laughter. "Ah, Polyphemus, stay off the wine." And they disappeared into the night.

"Don't think you're getting away that easily, Nobody!" said the giant. "I'll let my sheep go outside and then I'll find you in this cave. And don't think you can sneak out with the sheep. Maybe I can't see, but I can still FEEL the difference between a man

and a sheep!"

The giant rolled the huge stone aside and the flock of sheep trotted towards the entrance. As each sheep passed by him, Polyphemus felt it with his massive giant hands, to make sure it wasn't a sailor sneaking past him.

But Odysseus being the smarty skirt (no pants in Ancient Greece, remember) that he was, told his men to hang on *underneath* the sheep, so the Cyclops wouldn't feel them.

One by one, hanging beneath their sheep, Odysseus and his crew escaped into the night.

They ran down to the beach and swam out to their boat. Behind them, a huge angry roar came from the cave as the Cyclops realized he'd been tricked.

"I'll have my revenge on Nobody! Nobody tricks me! I mean… Nobody gets away… ah, you know what I mean!"

But even though he was super smart, Odysseus couldn't resist one final dig.

"Listen up, big guy!" Odysseus yelled back toward the beach. "It wasn't NOBODY that tricked you, but I, Odysseus—Smartest Guy in Ancient Greece. Woot!"

Polyphemus gnashed his teeth and hurled a giant boulder towards Odysseus.

"Oops," said Odysseus.

The massive rock crashed into the sea next to them, almost turning the ship over!

"Get rowing, crew!" shouted Odysseus. "He's going to throw another one!"

Baarbara, the new crew member, was already at the oars and bleating orders at the sailors.

"Wow!" said Odysseus. "That's one smart sheep. She'll go far."

"Let's hope she doesn't want to WOOL the world," said Barry with a grin.

Odysseus sighed and thought about pushing Barry overboard, but instead he went and had a cup of tea and a good lie down, because sometimes that's what smart people need to do.

CREW WANTED
Join an exciting life of sailing & adventure!
Great Benefits:
- See the World!
- Meet interesting people!
- Kill them!

DISCLAIMER
Crew members may be eaten by giants

HORSIN' AROUND: THE TROJAN WAR

Helen was the most beautiful woman in Greece.

She was stolen by a Trojan prince,

—LOOHODO

and taken to Troy.

TROY

This started a ten year war!

TROY IS TOPS

GREEKS R GREAT

Many great warriors including Achilles and Hector died.

But no matter how hard they tried, the Greeks couldn't enter the city of Troy.

Then Odysseus, a Greek general, had a brilliant plan...

They made a giant wooden horse, hid soldiers in it, and gave it to the Trojans as a present.

The Trojans loved the horse and dragged it into the city.

That night the soldiers hiding inside the Trojan Horse leapt out!

GREEKS		TROJANS
2	:	1

They opened the gate, the Greek army entered, and that was the end of Troy!

Tale the Sixth
Jason & the Farting Harpies
PART I

Jason, leader of the Argonauts was pretty grossed out. He'd seen a lot of icky stuff already on his voyage to capture the legendary Golden Fleece: flesh-eating giants, people getting drowned by water nymphs, Hercules's bum. But nothing had prepared him for this. Harpies. That's right. You heard. Harpies. The absolute worst dinner guests you can have. Ever.

CENSORED!
(Too Gross)

Do you have that friend that picks their nose and then wipes it on their sandwiches? That's not that gross.

Snot au vin

Or maybe your dad gets food stuck in his beard, and when you tell him, he picks it out and eats it? That's not that gross either.

Or your auntie, who every time you try to eat, she farts really, really smelly farts on your food? Yes? Well, that is gross and you should ask her to leave immediately because SHE IS OBVIOUSLY A HARPY BECAUSE THAT'S WHAT HARPIES DO! THEY FART AND FART WHENEVER YOU ARE EATING! Not by accident either. They mean it.

THE HUNGRY CYCLOPS
— BUFFET — NO HARPIES!*
*The Hungry Cyclops is a Fart-Free establishment.

Whatever you do, DO NOT INVITE A HARPY TO DINNER unless you're a major fan of fart salad. (And to be honest, how would you even eat fart salad?)

SPECIAL
Harpy Fart
Salad

FREE
NOSE STRAW
with purchase

Jason and his crew had set out on their quest months and months ago. He'd put together an absolutely top-notch crew for the trip—Hercules, Theseus, Achilles, Castor and his brother Pollux, Atalanta the Huntress. The list went on. Anyone who was anyone was there. There was a two-monster-slaying minimum just to get on the wait list. They had a talking boat, the Argo, and a cool name for the gang: The Argonauts!

What? Haven't seen a talking boat before?

Bon Voy
ARGO

108

But it had been a very long trip with lots of adventures, and all they wanted now was a rest. So when they passed the island of Bosporus, they decided to stop at the local castle for a bite to eat.

All You Can't Eat

The castle door creaked open, and out shuffled an incredibly thin old man. His legs were like a piece of spaghetti split in half, and he held on to the door tightly, in case a light breeze sprung up and blew him away. He stared from the door with only empty sockets where his eyes should be. He was blind.

"Greetings," said the man. "I have seen the future and know you are the Argonauts. You are most welcome here. I am King Phineus."

"More like King SKINNEUS!" roared Hercules, waving his hand around for a high five. "Amiright?! Amiright?!"

"Dude!" whispered Jason to Hercules. "Not cool!"

"Don't worry, Jase," said Hercules. "He can't hear us. He's blind."

"What? That's not what blind means. Seriously, how do you get through life?"

"No, no," interrupted the king, "your friend is quite right. Except about the blind thing. That's just stupid. But I am skinny, for I have not eaten for a long, long time."

Jason looked around the island. He could see herds of cows and fields of wheat. There didn't seem to be any shortage of food.

"So it's a diet thing?" he said. "Well, it's totally working. You look fabulous."

"It's not a diet," snapped the king. "Just come in for dinner, and you'll see what I mean."

The Argonauts sat down in a huge hall. Servants came out carrying huge plates piled high with delicious food: roast beef, baked potatoes, smoked chicken—you name it. The Argonauts licked their lips and slapped their bellies.

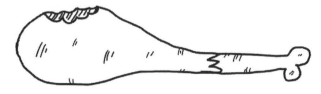

"2, 4, 6, 8!" shouted Hercules, grabbing a giant turkey leg, "Dig in, don't wa—"

SCREEEEEEEEEEECH!!!!

A hideous noise split the air! A dozen huge birds came shrieking and flapping down the chimney and into the room. No! Not birds—women! But with wings—HARPIES! Yes, that's right! HARPIES! Huge ugly heads filled with savage teeth! Wings tipped with razor-sharp claws! Pointy noses full of boogers! HORRIBLE! They screeched and shrieked as they flew around the room, making such a racket that the Argonauts clapped their hands over their ears in pain. But there was worse to come...

PHFFFFFFFFFFFFFFFFFFFFFFFFFFFFKAPOW!

A HUGE FART ripped through the room, flipping over tables and smashing the chairs to pieces. And did it smell? OH, YOU HAVE NO IDEA! It was like a million mushed-up rotten eggs! It was like a gazillion tonnes of the smelliest cheese ever! It was like your dad's socks! YES, IT WAS THAT BAD!

PLLPHHT!

The Harpies swooped and dove through the air, letting out a rat-a-tat-tat of stinky bottom burps, smelly butt belches, and toxic trouser coughs. All the delicious food shriveled on the plates. The Argonauts dove under the tables to take shelter from the giant fart storm. (A fartnado if you will.)

Out of farts and satisfied they had ruined all the food, the Harpies cackled an evil laugh and flew back up the chimney.

Hercules stared at the turkey leg in his hand. It was green and blistered and smelled so, so bad. He shrieked and dropped it.

"I almost put this in my mouth!" he gasped. "Imagine if I hadn't been looking? I could've eaten fart!"

"So," said King Phineus with a sour smile, "now you see why I'm so skinny."

END OF PART I

BAD ANCIENT GREEK JOKES

What is a Greek monster's favorite musical instrument?

The Harpy.

What did the Ancient Greeks wear on their feet?

Tennis Zeus

Who was the politest Greek god?

Apollo, 'cos he was always a pollo-gizing.

SCREEEECH!

What is a favorite game of the Ancient Greeks?

Hydra and go seek

Which Greek god farts the most?

Ares

Where did the Greeks get the Trojan Horse from?

Troys 'R' Us

TROYS 'R' US

Jason & the Farting Harpies
PART II

"I haven't eaten in months!" cried the king. "If there's food on the table, those Harpies come shrieking in and fart all over it."

Jason scratched his chin, thinking hard. "We could fight them for you," he said. "Bring them down with arrows."

THE FART OF WAR

by Sun Pew

FFFOOOMM!

"Tried that," said the king. "They just fart them out of the air."

"Could you learn to like farts?" asked Hercules. King Phineus glared at him. (Which is pretty hard to do when you've got no eyeballs.)

"Just a suggestion," muttered Hercules, sulkily.

The Tell Tale Fart

A Whodunnit? mystery

Edgar Allen Poo

Jason stared at his crew. Before him stood the greatest heroes in Ancient Greece. But they were tired, hungry, and smelled of farts. It was time for some stirring words to lift their spirits.

"Argonauts!" Jason said in his best, deepest, and loudest leader's voice. "Today, our quest stands upon a knife's edge. If we are to overcome this terrible challenge, then we must stand together as heroes! Once and for all—"

BLLLTTTPHFFFFRRRRRP!!!

A huge rumbling shook the palace!

"What on earth was that?" gasped Jason. "Some other terrible beast?"

Wasn't me.

"Umm, no," said Castor, one of the Argonauts, "that was me. Sorry. It's just that when my tummy gets empty, I get all gassy. I can't help it, sorry. My brother Pollux is the same."

"Yeah," said Pollux, his cheeks bulging, his face extremely red, "and I've been holding one in for ages."

"Could you maybe just wait till you're outsi—"

BRRRRRPPLLLTTT

BRRRRRPPP

PFFFFTTTT

BAAARR

Signed in as:
FartWarrior99

FARTNITE

A multi-smeller game

LOGGING IN...

RRRPPPPP

PPPRRRRRPPPPPPP!

116

Pollux's fart shook the room worse than Castor's!
Windows rattled and plates fell off the tables.

"Impressive," said Jason. "But I don't think it will help beat
the Harp—"

Then came the smell. BLLLEEEARRRRGHGGGH!!

Immediately, the Argonauts fell to the floor, gasping and
gagging. Achilles was under the table crying. Theseus
vomited into his helmet.

"Crack a window!" screamed Jason. "For
the love of Zeus, crack a window!"

Hercules threw his mighty club at the
door and smashed it open. A gust of fresh air began to
clear the evil funk from the room.

"Wow!" choked Jason once it was safe to
breathe again. "You two should be classed
as chemical weapons!"

"We're the sons of the North Wind," said Castor. "Dad calls us his little South Winds."

"That's some South Wind you've got there, all right" muttered Hercules. "Nothing could stand that."

"Indeed," said Jason slowly. He turned to the king. "Do you have any clothes pins by chance?"

The king nodded with a puzzled look.

"Then," said Jason with a wide grin, "I think it's time for dessert".

Minutes later, the Argonauts stood ready, their noses pinned shut and all the doors and windows sealed up. Jason gave the signal. The king clapped his hands and immediately servants rushed in with the best cakes, brownies, puddings, and ice creams ever.

Once more the Harpies came howling and farting into the room. But this time the Argonauts were ready.

"Castor! Pollux!" commanded Jason. "Bottoms at the ready… FIRE!"

The twins, on their hands and knees, flipped their togas up and LET RIP!

Ancient Greek Fart Cannon

The Harpies were hit full blast with the toxic gases of Castor and Pollux. They choked and gasped, feathers fell off their wings, one of them lost all control, whizzed round the room, did a somersault and smacked into the roof.

"That is DISGUSTING!" shrieked a Harpy. "And I should know, I fart on food for a living!"

"You're not going to get away with that!" barked the lead Harpy. "Ladies! It's time for Shock and Phwoaahhr!"

The flock of Harpies formed into a tight pack. As one, they turned their feathery butts towards the Argonauts and let out a single GIGANTIC butt sneeze.

The giant mushroom cloud of Harpy fart rolled towards the Argonauts. Glasses shattered! The floor cracked! The smell took all the curls out of Hercules's hair!

The foul-smelling tidal wave drew ever closer! But Jason held his nerve (and his nose).

"Sons of the North Wind," he said in a steely voice. "Your time is now. Fart like you have never farted before! BOTH BARRELS!"

Castor and Pollux bent over. They blasted the biggest-bottom ripping, butt-burning stink torpedoes they could. The two clouds of toxic gas crashed into each other! The earth trembled with the force of the giant FARTQUAKE! *KABOOM!* The roof blew off the castle! But the lethal bottom burps of Castor and Pollux were too strong for the Harpies! Their stinky stench cut through the toxic cloud, and *BOOM!* the Harpies were blown up, up and away into the skies, never to be seen again.

"Finally!" gasped King Phineus. "We can eat in peace."

"Now, that," said Jason with a grin, "is music to my ears."

120

"DON'T you mean," said Hercules, pointing at Castor and Pollux, "music FROM THEIR REARS!? BWAAAAHAHAHAAAAAAA!" Hercules slapped his thighs, laughing hysterically at his own joke.

"That's not funny," said Jason sternly. "Those monsters were dangerous."

"Here's another monster," roared Hercules, lifting his leg, *PFFFTT!* He let out a tiny little wheezing fart.

Castor smirked. Pollux snorted a giggle. Atalanta bit her bow to stop laughing. Even King Phineus started to chuckle. Then all the Argonauts were rolling about giggling, laughing, and gasping for breath.

Jason sighed. It was going to be a long, long trip.

YOU'VE DONE IT!

MASHED MYTHS
UNIVERSITY

_____
(your name here)

Has earned the award of
Ancient Greek Hero-ologist!

_____
Date

Congratulations! Against incredible odds and endless
distractions you've read this book! What a hero!!!!

You are now a 117% fully certified
ANCIENT GREEK HERO-OLOGIST
Well done Champ!

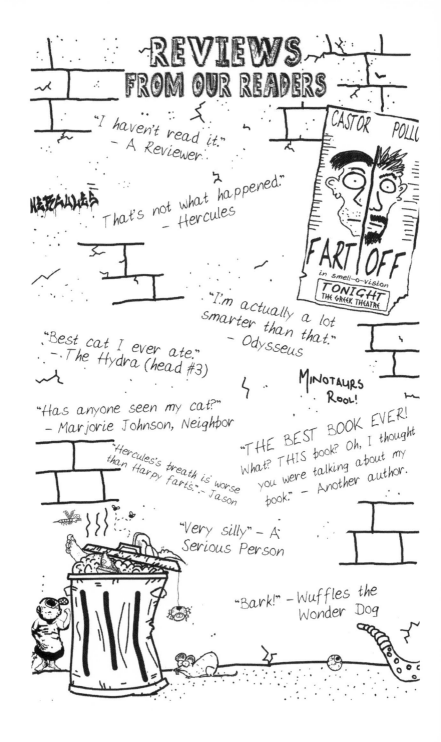

REVIEWS FROM OUR READERS

"I haven't read it."
— A Reviewer

"That's not what happened."
— Hercules

CASTOR POLL...

FART OFF
in smell-o-vision
TONIGHT
THE GREEK THEATRE

"I'm actually a lot smarter than that."
— Odysseus

"Best cat I ever ate."
— The Hydra (head #3)

MINOTAURS ROOL!

"Has anyone seen my cat?"
— Marjorie Johnson, Neighbor

"Hercules's breath is worse than Harpy farts." - Jason

"THE BEST BOOK EVER! What? THIS book? Oh, I thought you were talking about my book." — Another author.

"Very silly" — A Serious Person

"Bark!" — Wuffles the Wonder Dog

THE REAL TALES

Want to read the Ancient Myths BEFORE
they were mashed? Go to

www.mashedmyths.com

where you'll find all the original stories!

MORE STUFF!

Can't get enough Mashed Myths? Well, here's some
stuff you can do until the next book comes out!

*Mash a myth yourself! That's right!
Take any ancient myth and
GO CRAZY!

*Write your own myth
(with you as the hero!)

*Design a suit of armor!

*Invent a monster!

*Draw a comic about your
favorite ancient hero!

And for even more ideas, check out our website
www.mashedmyths.com

A special Mashed thanks

We'd love to thank everyone who supported us during the making of this book. There are way too many people to name individually, but we are very, VERY grateful to you all. We'd especially like to thank all the children and teachers at the many schools that gave us their fantastic feedback and laughter.

And finally thanks to our families for not only their incredible love and support, but for putting up with hundreds of stupid questions about Greek heroes and endless bad jokes.

Mick & Andrew